S0-EKZ-968

DELETE THIS BOOK
from Jerabek School Library

AlphaBasiCs

The Wonders of Me

from A to Z

A Bobbie Kalman Book

 Crabtree Publishing Company

AlphaBasiCs

Created by Bobbie Kalman

For Ross Vernal
and his two "wonders"

Editor-in-Chief
Bobbie Kalman

Writing team
Bobbie Kalman
Niki Walker

Managing editor
Lynda Hale

Editors
Niki Walker
Greg Nickles

Computer design
Lynda Hale

Production coordinator
Hannelore Sotzek

Separations and film
Dot 'n Line Image Inc.

Printer
Worzalla Publishing Company

Special thanks to
Allison and Amanda Vernal; Nicola Hill; Samantha Crabtree;
Ramona Gellel and the students of Precious Blood School;
Katie Prosper; Elia Sadil; Johnathan Sacitharah; Bryn Mercer;
Victor Qundos; Darrick Yu; Hilary Kuzmaski; the students of
Michael J. Brennan and Pine Grove Elementary Schools;
Al Spicer and the West Lincoln Memorial Hospital

Photographs
Marc Crabtree: pages 14, 21, 27
Christl Hill: page 7 (both)
Bobbie Kalman: pages 4, 9, 10 (all), 11 (top left),
    22 (bottom left), 23 (bottom right), 26, 30
Jerry Whitaker: page 29
Other photographs by Digital Stock, Digital Vision,
    and Image Club Graphics

Illustrations
Antoinette "Cookie" Bortolon: pages 5, 11, 19
Deborah Drew-Brook-Cormack: page 13

Crabtree Publishing Company

350 Fifth Avenue
Suite 3308
New York
N.Y. 10118

360 York Road, RR 4
Niagara-on-the-Lake
Ontario, Canada
L0S 1J0

73 Lime Walk
Headington
Oxford OX3 7AD
United Kingdom

Copyright © **1998 CRABTREE PUBLISHING COMPANY**.
All rights reserved. No part of this publication may be reproduced,
stored in a retrieval system or be transmitted in any form or by
any means, electronic, mechanical, photocopying, recording, or
otherwise, without the prior written permission of Crabtree
Publishing Company.

Cataloging in Publication Data
Kalman, Bobbie
    The wonders of me from A to Z
(AlphaBasiCs)
Includes index.
ISBN 0-86505-375-8 (library bound) ISBN 0-86505-405-3 (pbk.)
This alphabet book introduces aspects associated with human
development, relationships, and personality, such as friendship,
imagination, talents, and the human body.

1. Child development—Juvenile literature. 2. Child psychology—
Juvenile literature. 3. Body, Human—Juvenile literature. 4. English
language—Alphabet—Juvenile literature. [1. Child development.
2. Psychology. 3. Body, Human. 4. Alphabet.] I. Title. II. Series:
Kalman, Bobbie. AlphaBasiCs.

HQ767.9.K35 1997   j305.235′5   LC 97-34893
                                                            CIP

CONTENTS

is for **alive**. I am a living thing. Birds, squirrels, flowers, and trees are some other living things. I need to breathe air, drink water, and eat food. Air, food, and water give me energy and keep my body alive. Some of the things in this picture are alive. Some aren't. Which five things are alive? Which five things are not?

is for **body**. My body is made up of many different parts. You can see some parts, like my skin, hair, and face. My bones and muscles are under my skin. You can't see them! My brain is in my head. It is one of my most important parts. I use it to think and remember things. My brain also tells my body what to do.

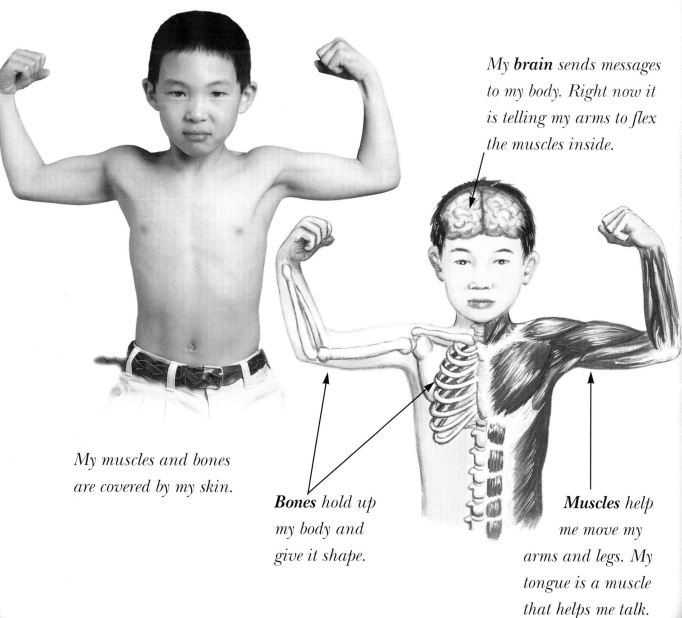

*My **brain** sends messages to my body. Right now it is telling my arms to flex the muscles inside.*

My muscles and bones are covered by my skin.

***Bones** hold up my body and give it shape.*

***Muscles** help me move my arms and legs. My tongue is a muscle that helps me talk.*

is for **clothes**. Clothes help protect me from the sun, wind, and rain. When it is cold outside, I wear a sweater and coat. I also put on a hat and mittens. When it is hot, I wear shorts and a tee shirt. Sometimes I dress like a grown-up for fun. My favorite clothes are my jeans and striped sweater. Which are yours?

I love dressing up in my mom's clothes, but it's hard to walk in her shoes!

is for **dreams**. Dreams are like movies that play in my mind when I sleep. Some dreams are about things that have happened. Some are like amazing adventures. Once in a while, I have a **nightmare**. I'm always happy to wake up from one of those scary dreams! What is the best dream you've ever had?

*Sometimes I **daydream**. I daydream when I'm awake. Right now I'm daydreaming about what it would be like to have a pony.*

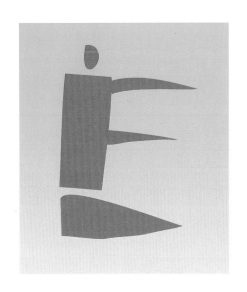

is for **emotions**. Emotions are also called **feelings**. I can feel sad, scared, angry, embarrassed, happy, or excited. We all feel different emotions for different reasons. What makes you feel sad, happy, nervous, or angry? Make up a story about the children below. What do you think each one is feeling? Why?

EXCITED EMBARRASSED NERVOUS DISAPPOINTED BORED JEALOUS ANGRY HAPPY SAD AFRAID

is for **friends**. My friends are people who like me. I like them, too. We have fun talking and playing together. My friends never ask me to do things that might hurt me. They don't make fun of me. They make me feel good about myself! We don't always agree, but we try to **compromise** instead of fighting.

ACCEPTANCE SMILES COMPROMISE
CARING SHARING
GAMES
LOVE
HELP
LAUGHTER
FUN TALKS
SUPPORT

is for **growing**. All living things grow. They grow bigger, and they grow older. I was a tiny baby when I was born. My body has grown and changed a lot since then! I have grown taller, and I don't look the same. My mind has grown, too. I can learn more, and I can do many things I couldn't do when I was small.

This is me when I was one year and eight years old. I'm 19 years old now.

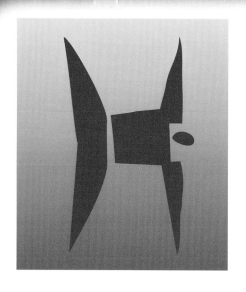

is for **hair**. You may see only the hair on my head, but hair grows almost everywhere on my body. Look at your legs, toes, fingers, and face. I bet you have hair on your body just like I do! Hair is made by our skin. Skin is "alive," but hair isn't, so it doesn't hurt to have it cut. Hair can be curly, straight, or wavy.

Hair is straight, wavy, or curly because of the way it is shaped. Straight hair strands are round. Wavy strands are oval. Curly strands of hair are shaped like jelly beans.

is for **imagination**. My imagination helps me solve problems. I also use my imagination when I talk or play. I have fun when I use it to make up stories and draw pictures. When I paint, my imagination tells me how the picture will look. I see the picture in my mind, and then I use paint to put my idea on paper.

is for **jealousy**. Jealousy is an emotion that I don't like. When my baby brother was born, my mom spent all her time with him. I worried that she didn't love me anymore, and I was angry at the baby. I didn't like feeling jealous, so I tried playing with him. Now I love my brother! Have you felt jealous? When?

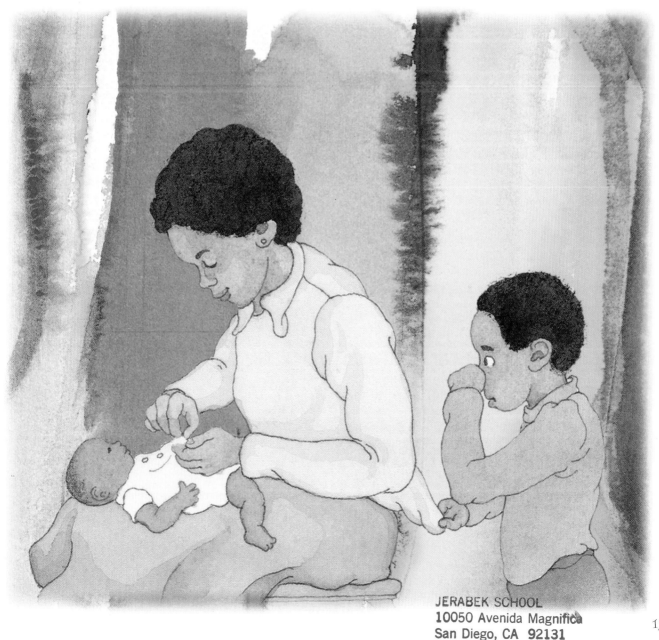

JERABEK SCHOOL
10050 Avenida Magnifica
San Diego, CA 92131
578-5330

is for **know**. I know my address and my phone number. Do you know yours? I know all the kids in my class. Who are some people you know? I also know how to do things. I know how to use a computer. I know how to swim, in-line skate, and ride my bike. What are some things that you know how to do?

is for **laugh**. Laughing jiggles my body. It is good for me. Jokes and funny stories make me laugh. I laugh when I see someone making a silly face. Sometimes I laugh just because I see other people laughing. I don't laugh at other people, though. I don't like it when someone laughs at my mistakes or the way I look!

M is for **moods**. Moods are feelings that last for awhile. I may get into a mood because of something someone says or does. Sometimes I wake up in a great mood for no

CREATIVE

PLAYFUL

GROUCHY

QUIET

reason at all. Other times I feel grumpy all day. I have a lot of moods. Sometimes I'm in the mood to play hide and seek!

THOUGHTFUL

SILLY

GRUMPY

ADVENTUROUS

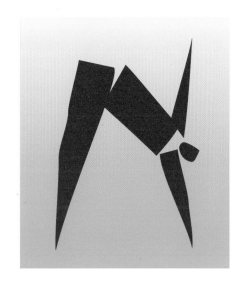

is for **noises**. My body makes all kinds of loud and funny noises. They are almost always a surprise! I sneeze, cough, and get the hiccups. My stomach makes rumbling sounds when I'm hungry. Sometimes I snore when I'm sleeping. My sister hates it! What are some of the sounds your body makes?

"Excuse me!"

is for **organs**. Organs are parts of my body that have important jobs to do. I have many different organs. Organs such as my brain, heart, and lungs keep me alive. They are my **vital organs**. My eyes and ears let me know what is happening around me. They are **sense organs**.

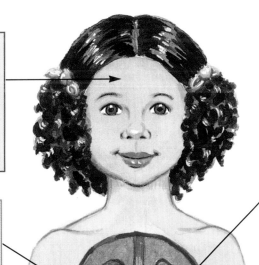

My brain controls all the parts of my body that keep me alive. It makes my heart beat and my lungs breathe.

My lungs help my body get the oxygen it needs to stay alive.

My liver helps my body digest food. It also cleans my blood.

Skin is my body's largest organ! It protects my insides from heat, cold, dirt, and germs.

My heart is very strong. It pumps blood around my body, from the top of my head to the tip of my toes.

My stomach mashes the food I swallow into a soupy liquid.

The liquid moves to my intestines. My intestines take energy and nutrients from the liquid.

is for **playing**. I love playing! It's a lot of fun, and it's also good for me. Playing uses my imagination. I can play games and pretend to be anything I choose. Playing sports exercises my heart, lungs, arms, and legs and makes them stronger. I have fun playing games with my friends, but I really love playing with my dog!

is for **quarrels**. Quarrels are arguments. Sometimes I quarrel with my friends about the games we're going to play. Sometimes we quarrel because one of us won't share. We yell and say mean things. I don't like quarreling with my friends. It isn't fun, and it makes both of us feel bad.

R is for **relatives**. Relatives are the people in my family. My parents, grandparents, brothers and sisters, aunts and uncles, and cousins are my relatives. Some of my relatives live with me. Others live far away. I like making trips to visit them. Who are your relatives? Where do they live?

(top left) My mom married Jack's dad two years ago. Jack is my stepbrother. His dad is my stepdad.
(left) Last year I visited my relatives in Israel. I met my new baby cousin.
(above) My little sister loves me very much. She looks up to me.

is for **senses**. I have five senses. I **see** colors and shapes with my eyes. I **hear** all kinds of sounds with my ears. I **taste** sweet, sour, bitter, and salty things with my tongue. I **smell** things with my nose. I can **touch** things and tell if they feel soft, hard, smooth, or scratchy. I also feel things like tickles and itches on my skin.

(above) Watermelon tastes great! Sweet foods are my favorite. What's your favorite taste?
(top right) When I pet my cat, I feel her soft fur and hear her purring.
(right) Colorful flowers look beautiful, and they smell wonderful!

is for **talents**. The things that I do well are my talents. I'm talented at swimming, taking pictures, and drawing. I'm also good at telling jokes and making people laugh. I can't play basketball well, but my

friend Josh can. We all do some things better than we do others. The talents we have help make us special. What are your talents?

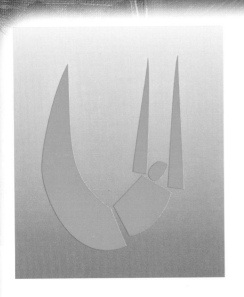

is for **unique**. Unique means different and special. Everyone is unique. Some of us are tall, and others are short. Some have dark skin, and others are light-skinned. Some people are good at sports, and others aren't. It's great to be unique! Imagine how boring life would be if we looked alike and had the same talents.

All the children in this picture are different in many ways. Write down ten things that make you unique. Which things do you like best about yourself?

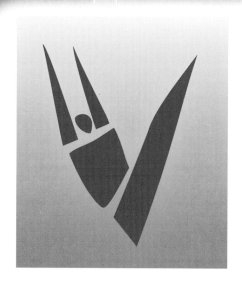

is for **vocabulary**. My vocabulary is all the words I know. I learn at least one new word every day, so I have a big vocabulary. Knowing words means I can spell them correctly. I recognize them when I see them in books. I also know what the words mean. I keep learning more words so that my vocabulary will grow.

To make your vocabulary grow, read a lot of books! When you find a word you don't know, look it up in a dictionary. Use the word in three sentences and you won't forget what it means.

is for **weight**. When I stand on a scale, I can tell how heavy or light I am. The scale shows how much I weigh. Water makes up more than half my weight! It is in every part of my body. I have weight because of **gravity**. It pulls me towards the earth. When I jump over my pool, gravity pulls me down into the water. Splash!

is for **x-ray**. An x-ray is a way of seeing inside my body. Seeing inside my body helps doctors know if I am healthy. An x-ray shows them my bones or my teeth. When I fell off my bike, my doctor took an x-ray of my arm to see if any bones were broken. The x-ray in the picture shows the bones in my arm and hand.

is for **yawn**. A yawn is a long, deep breath. I yawn when I'm tired. I also yawn after sitting still for a long time. When I yawn, it means my body needs more oxygen. I don't have to think about yawning. It just happens. Sometimes I wish I could stop yawning! My teacher thinks I'm bored when I yawn in class.

is for "catching my **ZZZs**," or sleeping. Sleep gives my body a chance to rest. After being busy all day, I need to sleep. My teddy needs to sleep, too. I don't always feel like going to bed at my bedtime, but I know what happens if I don't get enough sleep. I wake up in the morning feeling tired and grumpy!

WORDS TO KNOW

acceptance The state of being liked or received in a friendly way

adventurous Describing a person who enjoys trying new and exciting activities

compromise To give in a little in order to settle an argument

creative Describing a person who has the ability to make new things

digest To break down food so that the body can use it for energy

embarrass To make someone feel uncomfortable and nervous or ashamed

emotion A feeling, such as anger, sadness, or happiness

energy The strength or desire to work or play

gravity The force that keeps things on the earth's surface and causes things thrown in the air to fall to the ground

imagination The ability of the mind to form pictures and to make up things that did not really happen

muscle A type of body tissue that makes body parts move

nervous Describing a person who is easily excited or upset

nutrient A substance in food that is needed by the body in order to stay healthy

oxygen A colorless gas in the air that all animals need to breathe to stay alive

support To provide with care, help, or comfort; also to agree with

talent A special natural ability to do something well

thoughtful Describing a person who shows care and consideration for others

INDEX

1 2 3 4 5 6 7 8 9 0   Printed in the U.S.A.   6 5 4 3 2 1 0 9 8 7